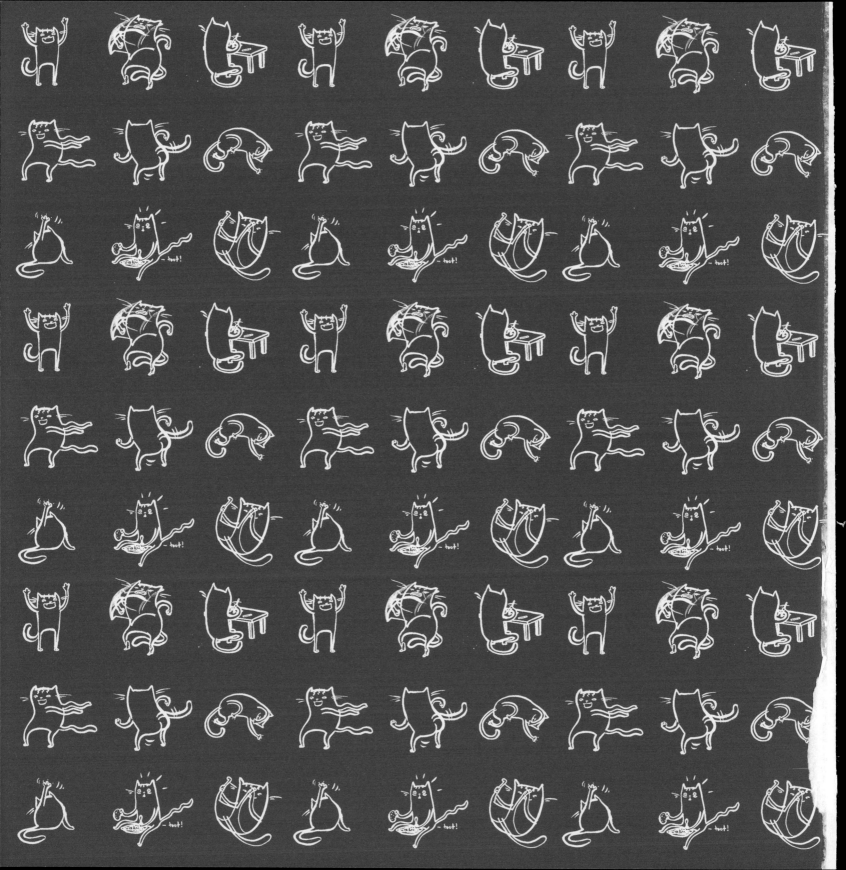

I AM DOODLE CAT

Kat Patrick & Lauren Marriott

I am Doodle Cat

I AM DOODLE CAT

Kat Patrick & Lauren Marriott

I AM DOODLE CAT

Kat Patrick & Lauren Marriott

SCRIBBLE

I only know
what I

love

I love

dancing

I love noise

I love the ocean

I love farts

I love ice cream

I love friends

I love trees

2 PEGS + 1 CHIP
I FOUND IN THE
COUCH

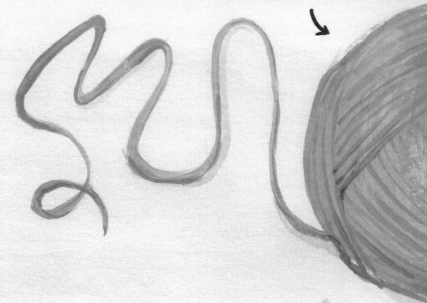

I love

+ 3 BIRDS

- 2 HAIR
BALLS

× 2.5 WORMING
TABLETS I PRETENDED
TO SWALLOW

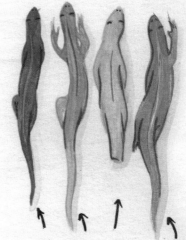

÷ BY 11 FISH-SHAPED BISCUITS

+ 4 THIN LIZZIES

↓

- 1 TAIL

maths

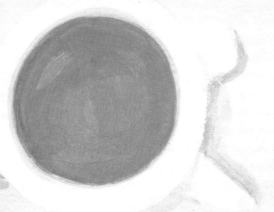

+ MY SHADES

+2 TOY MICE

- 2 BABY TEETH

I love lentils

I love baths

I love

this

rug

I love fractals

I love my onesie

I love small animals

I love the stars

I love doodling

I love going fast

I love
difference

I am
Doodle Cat

I love me!

What do
you love?

I love the ocean.
The ocean is one big, beautiful mystery. It covers 70% of the earth's surface, and we haven't even met half the creatures that call it home. Whoa, imagine what pals are left for us to meet!

I love farts.
Our bodies are quite clever. The average person produces half a litre of farts every day and it's not just humans that do it. Termites are officially the fartiest animals on the planet. Bet they do small ones, though.

I love friends.
My best friend is a Pangolin. He's from Africa. He's a mammal, like you and me, and he's covered in clever scales. Cool guy. Makes hugging a little scratchy, though.

I love trees.
Trees make oxygen for us to breathe, have big leaves for us to make into excellent headdresses and decent branches for climbing. Good places to dream up big ideas.

I love fractals.

A fractal is a never-ending pattern that looks exactly the same at any size. These guys are everywhere! Don't believe me? Go and investigate a cauliflower.

I love the stars.

Scientists put the stars in different groups: Red Dwarfs, Giant Stars, Blue Giant Stars, Super Giant Stars, and Yellow Stars. I think that if I were a star I would be a Red Dwarf.

I love difference.

Difference keeps us interesting. If we were all the same, we'd have nothing to say to each other. Imagine just staring at the mirror all day. Boring.

I love me!

It's very important to love you. Because you really are pretty great. Don't believe me? Start a list of all the things that you love, and all the things you like best about yourself. Then send it to me. Paw-five!

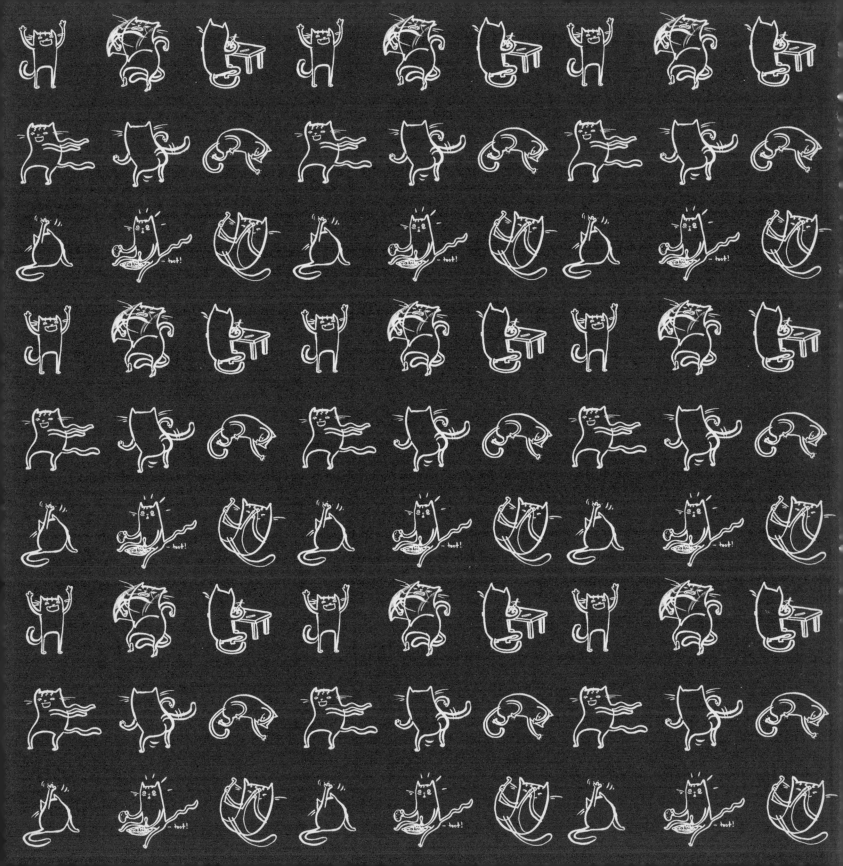